The Wheels on the Bus USA: Alabama

Ashley Goodsell

Copyright © 2022 Ashley Goodsell

All rights reserved.

ISBN: 9798841649106

DEDICATION

To my children who love the song Wheels on the Bus and my husband, Ryan, who came up with silly versus and encouraged me in my writing

The wheels on the bus go round and round,

Round and round,

Round and round.

The wheels on the bus go round and round,

All through Alabama.

Hank Aaron on the bus says play baseball,

Play baseball,

Play baseball.

Hank Aaron on the bus says play baseball,

All through Alabama.

Harper Lee on the bus says read more books,

Read more books,

Read more books.

Harper Lee on the bus says read more books,

All through Alabama.

Rosa Parks on the bus says choose your seat,

Choose your seat,

Choose your seat.

Rosa Parks on the bus says choose your seat,

All through Alabama.

Mia Hamm on the bus says kick the ball,

Kick the ball,

Kick the ball.

Mia Hamm on the bus says kick the ball,

All through Alabama.

Carl Lewis on the bus says run your race,

Run your race,

Run your race.

Carl Lewis on the bus says run your race,

All through Alabama.

Jesse Owens on the bus says win the gold,

Win the gold,

Win the gold.

Jesse Owens on the bus says win the gold,

All through Alabama.

Helen Keller on the bus says don't give up,

Don't give up,

Don't give up.

Helen Keller on the bus says don't give up,

All through Alabama.

William Handy on the bus says play the blues,

Play the blues,

Play the blues.

William Handy on the bus says play the blues,

All through Alabama.

The wheels on the bus go round and round,

Round and round,

Round and round.

The wheels on the bus go round and round,

All through Alabama.

Henry "Hank" Aaron

February 5, 1934- January 22, 2021 (Mobile, Alabama)

Hank started his baseball career in 1951 by signing with the Indianapolis Clowns of the Negro American League, went on to sign with the Boston Braves, and in 1954 he signed on with the Milwaukee Braves. He hit a total of 755 home runs throughout his baseball career and was inducted into the National Baseball Hall of Fame in 1982.

Nelle Harper Lee

April 28, 1926- February 19, 2016 (Monroeville, Alabama)

This American novelist was born Monroeville, Alabama. In 1960, <u>To Kill a Mockingbird</u> was published and went on to be a best-selling and won Pulitzer Prize for Fiction. She published <u>Go Set a Watchman</u> in 2015, as a sequel to <u>To Kill a Mockingbird</u>.

Rosa Parks

February 4, 1913- October 24, 2005 (Tuskegee, Alabama)

Rosa was born in Tuskegee, Alabama. She was an African American activist in the civil rights movement and best known for her role in the Montgomery Bus Boycott in 1955. She refused to give up her bus seat to a while man and was arrested. She went on to be awarded the presidential Medal of Freedom, the Congressional Gold Medal, and more.

Mariel Margaret Hamm-Garciaparra

March 17, 1972-   (Selma, Alabama)

Mia was born in Selma, Alabama. She started her soccer career in 1989 by playing in college for North Carolina Tar Heels women's soccer team and helped the team win four NCAA Championships titles. She played for the U.S National team, competed in four FIFA Women's World Cup, and three Olympic Games. She retired from professional soccer in 2004. She was inducted into the National Soccer Hall of Fame in 2007 and the World Football Hall of Fame in 2013.

Frederick Carlton Lewis

July 1, 1961 –   (Birmingham, Alabama)

Carl Lewis is known for his track and field performances in the long jump and sprinting. He won 9 Olympic gold medals, 1 silver medal, and 10 world championship medals. He set the world record in the 100-meter sprint, 4x100 meter relay, and 4x200 meter relay. He has jumped just over 28 feet. In 1999, he was voted Sportsman of the Century and named World Athlete of the Century.

James "Jesse" Owens

September 12, 1913- March 31, 1980 (Oakville, Alabama)

Jesse was born in Oakville, Alabama. In 1935, he set 3 world records: long jump, 220-yard sprint, and 220-yard low hurdles. He also tied the 100-yard sprint that same time. He attended the 1936 Olympic games in Germany. He won 4 gold medals: 100-meter sprint, 200-meter sprint, 4x100 meter relay, and long jump. In 1979 he was awarded the Living Legend Award by President Jimmy Carter.

Helen Keller

June 27, 1880- June 1, 1968 (Tuscumbia, Alabama)

Born in Tuscumbia, Alabama. At the young age of 19 months, Helen lost her sight and hearing due to an illness. She went on to learn how to speak and to understand others as they spoke using the Tadema method. She attended Radcliffe College of Harvard and obtained a Bachelor's in Art. In 1961, President Johnson awarded her the Presidential Medal of Freedom. In 1965 Helen was elected to the National Women's Hall of Fame.

William Handy

November 16, 1873- March 28, 1958 (Florence, Alabama)

Handy is known as the "Father of Blues" as he was the first to publish music in the Blues form. In 1912, he published "Memphis Blues" and sold the rights to the song. He went on to compose many more songs, he is best known for his "St. Louis Blues". In 1970, he was inducted into Songwriters Hall of Fame.

Made in the USA
Middletown, DE
18 September 2022